I read this book all by myself

For Orlando – SK
For my Auntie Fran – LF

A TALE OF TWO WOLVES
A Red Fox Book: 0 09 943213 7

First published in Great Britain in 2002 by Red Fox
an imprint of Random House Children's Books

1 3 5 7 9 10 8 6 4 2

Text copyright © Susan Kelly 2002
Illustrations copyright © Lizzie Finlay 2002

The right of Susan Kelly and Lizzie Finlay to be identified as the author and
illustrator of this work has been asserted in accordance with the
Copyright, Designs and Patents Act, 1988.

Set in Cheltenham Book Infant

Red Fox Books are published by Random House Children's Books,
61–63 Uxbridge Road, London W5 5SA,
a division of The Random House Group Ltd,
in Australia by Random House Australia (Pty) Ltd,
20 Alfred Street, Milsons Point, Sydney, NSW 2061, Australia,
in New Zealand by Random House New Zealand Ltd,
18 Poland Road, Glenfield, Auckland 10, New Zealand,
and in South Africa by Random House (Pty) Ltd,
Endulini, 5A Jubilee Road, Parktown 2193, South Africa

THE RANDOM HOUSE GROUP Limited Reg. No. 954009
www.kidsatrandomhouse.co.uk

A CIP catalogue record for this book is available from the British Library.

Printed and bound in Singapore by Tien Wah Press

A Tale of Two Wolves

Susan Kelly   Lizzie Finlay

RED FOX

There was once a very good wolf and a very bad wolf. They were twins. They looked so alike that nobody could tell them apart. However, there was one difference . . .

The very bad wolf

The very good wolf

5

The very good wolf had two brown eyes,
while the very bad wolf had one brown eye
and one blue eye.

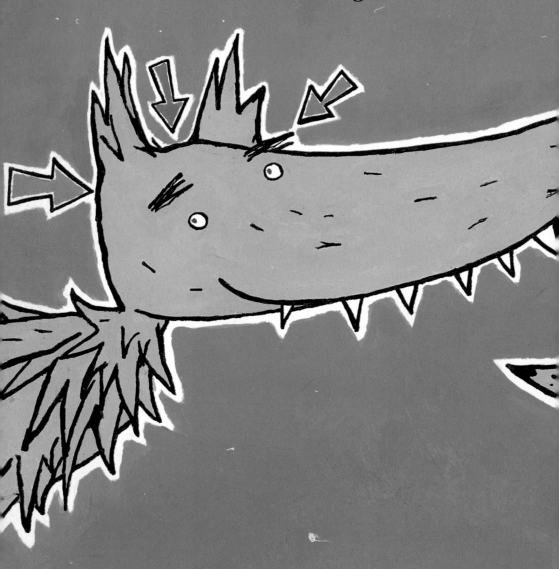

But it was a very small difference.

The very good wolf had not had a very good morning. First of all, he burnt his bottom getting into his bath, which had been much too hot for him.

And then he cut his tummy while giving himself a haircut.

He bandaged himself up with a huff and a puff and went back to bed. He was feeling very sorry for himself when there was a knock on the door.

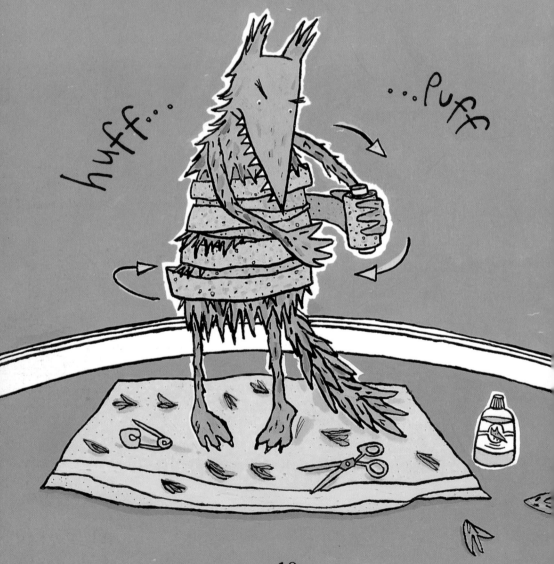

Two policemen were standing on his doorstep.

"We have been ordered to arrest you," they said.

They drove him off to the police station,

and locked him in a dark, damp cell.

...but ...but

A few days later, the very good wolf was taken to court. Everywhere people pushed to get a better view of him. Reporters scrambled to get a good photo. Nobody noticed the very bad wolf hiding in the background.

"Mr Wolf," the judge began, "we are here today to decide if you are guilty or not guilty."

JUDGE

The very good wolf looked around him
and gulped.

"Do you plead guilty or not guilty?"
asked the judge.

"Not guilty," replied the very good wolf
nervously.

"I understand you have chosen not to get a lawyer to defend you," said the judge. "You say you can speak for yourself?"

The very good wolf nodded.

"Very well," said the judge, "let us begin!"

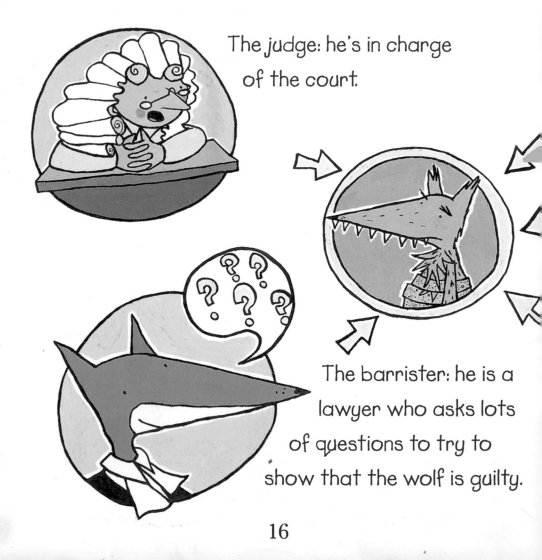

The judge: he's in charge of the court.

The barrister: he is a lawyer who asks lots of questions to try to show that the wolf is guilty.

The public: they watch from the gallery.

The jury: they listen carefully and decide
what will happen.

The witnesses: they tell everyone what they've seen.

The press: they report what is happening.

"You seem to have been in the wars,"
began the barrister. "How did you get that
nasty burn on your bottom?"

"I had an accident getting into my bath,"
replied the very good wolf, blushing.

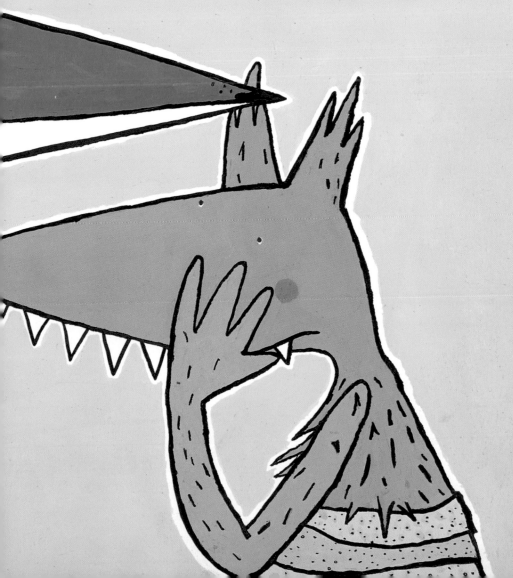

"Is that so?" said the barrister, raising his eyebrows. "Please could my first witnesses, the Three Little Pigs, trot forward."

"Have you seen this wolf before?" asked the barrister.

"Yes, he blew down my straw house!" cried the first little pig.

"And then my stick house!" cried the second little pig.

"But not my brick house!" cried the third little pig.

The crowd cheered.

"And it was at this brick house that you laid a trap for him?" asked the barrister.

"Yes, he fell down my chimney into a pot of boiling water and burnt his big hairy bottom. Then he ran off howling," said the third little pig.

"And are you sure it is the same wolf?" asked the barrister.

"Oh, yes!" squealed the little pigs.

"But . . . but . . ." cried the very good wolf.

But the barrister ignored him.

"Thank you, pigs. You may sit down. And what about that cut on your tummy?" the barrister continued. "How did that happen?"

"I was trimming my fur when I cut my tummy," replied the very good wolf.

"How interesting," said the barrister. "Please could the woodcutter come forward."

"Have you seen this wolf before?" asked the barrister.

"Yes. This is the wolf who gobbled up my daughter, Little Red Riding Hood, and her grandmother," said the woodcutter. "I cut open his big hairy tummy with my axe to let them out. Then he ran away screaming."

"And you are sure this is the same wolf?"

"Oh, yes," said the woodcutter.

"But . . . but . . . " cried the very good wolf.

But the barrister ignored him.

"Thank you, woodcutter. Finally, can the Three Bears come forward," said the barrister. "You were out walking in the woods when you saw this wolf talking to Little Red Riding Hood?"

"Yes, we were waiting for our porridge to cool down," said Mummy Bear.

"And you are sure it's the same wolf?"

"Oh, yes!" growled the Three Bears.

"But . . . but . . ." cried the very good wolf.

But the barrister ignored him.

... But ...but!

We'd recognise his big hairy ears any day.

"I have no more questions," said the barrister.

"Thank you," said the judge. "What say the jury?"

The jury whispered amongst themselves.
Everyone held their breath and waited.

Finally, a member of the jury stepped
forward and cried out, "GUILTY!"
The courtroom cheered.

Suddenly a little girl in a red riding hood made her way to the front.

"Excuse me," she said to the judge, "but you have the wrong wolf."

The courtroom fell silent.
"What do you mean, child?"
asked the judge.

"When I said to the wolf in my granny's bed, 'Oh what big eyes you've got', I noticed he had one big brown eye and one big blue eye."

Everyone gazed into the
very good wolf's two big brown
innocent eyes and gasped.

"The wolf who is guilty is standing right there at the back of the room," said Little Red Riding Hood. Everyone turned to see the very bad wolf trying to escape. He had a patch over one eye, and he was also covered in bandages.

After a few moments the judge shook his head and said, "We nearly made a terrible mistake today. But Little Red Riding Hood has taught us all an important lesson. And now the jury must decide how this tale is to end happily ever after . . ."

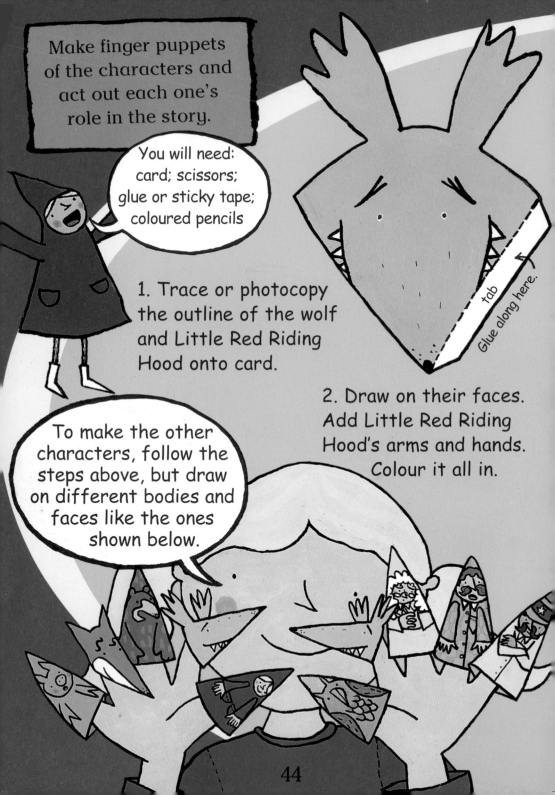

Make finger puppets of the characters and act out each one's role in the story.

You will need: card; scissors; glue or sticky tape; coloured pencils

1. Trace or photocopy the outline of the wolf and Little Red Riding Hood onto card.

tab

Glue along here.

2. Draw on their faces. Add Little Red Riding Hood's arms and hands. Colour it all in.

To make the other characters, follow the steps above, but draw on different bodies and faces like the ones shown below.

3. Cut out the characters (ask an adult to help). Fold them into a cone like this.

Glue along here.

tab

4. Stick the ends together with glue or sticky tape so that the tab goes inside the cone.

5. Now act out the story with your own ending.

If you were a member of the jury, what would you have done at the end of the story? Do you think Little Red Riding Hood was right to speak out?

There are twelve people on a jury. They decide if the person on trial is guilty or not.

Meet the author.

Susan Kelly

Where did you get the idea for this story? When I was studying fairy tales with my class of seven-year-olds, I remembered how scared I used to be of the Big Bad Wolf. So I decided to write a book about having him locked up, and here it is!

How long did it take you to write this story? I already had the story in my head, so my first draft only took about a day to write. I then made quite a few changes, which took longer.

What do you do if you get stuck on your writing? I go for a long walk and often new ideas suddenly come to me.

When you were little did you ever have to make difficult choices like the characters in this story? I remember when I was in trouble feeling it would be easier to lie than tell the truth. I soon learnt that little white lies can easily turn into bigger lies and you can end up in even bigger trouble.

Can I be a writer like you? Somebody once told me that everyone has a book inside their head. It was true for me and it could be true for you if you really want to write one.

Did you always want to be a writer? I used to love writing stories, but I really wanted to be a teacher more than anything.

Lizzie Finlay

Meet the illustrator.

What did you use to paint the pictures in this book? I used pencils, ink, acrylic paint and stacks and stacks of paper.

Did you paint the pictures all at once? First I drew the whole book out in rough, and then I changed lots of things. When I was happy with the pictures, I started painting. It has all taken about three months.

When you were little, did you ever have to make difficult choices like the characters in this story? I remember the first bit of money I owned. It was 50p to spend at a fairground and it felt like a very big deal at the time. I couldn't decide whether to keep it or to buy something. In the end I bought a toy monkey, but he wasn't as good as he looked on the stall.

Can I be an illustrator like you? Yes, just get drawing. You can be whatever you want to be! I feel really lucky to be doing the job I always wanted to do. I love it!

What gives you good ideas? I daydream a lot, and keep my eyes peeled for interesting people and animals. When you mix them up in your imagination, exciting things can happen.

Will you try and write or draw a story too?

47

Let your ideas take flight with
Flying Foxes